Missing

A DCI Rylan Crowe Mystery

Praise for Missing

"Missing" is a great story. Better than any episode of Law & Order I've ever seen."

— *dog-earred-reader (Barnes & Noble)*

"Missing" is a BritCrime adventure that leads the reader down a primrose path to a darker place where the unexpected and the unimaginable fight for equal space. Detective Chief Inspector Crowe is suave and smart, and the perfect guide for JM Reinbold's twisty tale about a lost child in a small English village."

-- *Ramona DeFelice Long*

"I thought I knew how it would end. Never in a million years could I have guessed. That was a good story!"

– *Unthula*

"…one of my top five favorite stories (in Someone Wicked)"

 – Dave Granger (Goodreads)

"Missing" by JM Reinbold - Gripping, terrifying and sad. This races down the halls of scary things.

– Art Griswald (Amazon)

"Some of my favorites were … "Missing" by JM Reinbold for setting and dialogue."

– Mark Taneyhill (Amazon)

My thought provoking favorites …. "Missing" by JM Reinbold.

– Frank Hopkins (Amazon)

JM Reinbold's "Missing" didn't miss at all. It hit the mark in so many ways. The story did not go anywhere I thought it would. When I was done, I wanted more of this one.

– Faithful85 (Barnes & Noble)

MISSING

A DCI RYLAN CROWE MYSTERY

BY JM REINBOLD

For Caroline Graham

MISSING

Detective Chief Inspector Rylan Crowe and Detective Sergeant Rolly Burke parked in front of the Mortimer house. The downstairs curtains were drawn, the drive empty.

Burke shut off the Ford Mondeo's engine. "No one home, looks like."

"They're at home," Crowe replied. He fished in his inside jacket pocket for a cigarette that wasn't there. "The shoe is Evie's. Smythe got confirmation from them not ten minutes ago." He hadn't smoked in a year or more, but with the clock ticking away on Evie Mortimer, the urge clawed at him, like he'd never quit. Haunted him like a ghost in his brain.

"I expect they've had more attention than they can bear. A missing child brings on the helpful and unhelpful in droves."

"No need to disturb them," Burke said. "For the moment."

"Right," Crowe agreed. "Smythe's volunteer is the first order of business."

They stepped from the car into a warm, pleasant morning. While London boiled in a July heat wave, Somerset and the rest of the Southwest enjoyed ocean breezes and temperatures in the mid-70s.

They found Detective Constable Smythe, the officer in charge of the grid search, in a portable pavilion set up inside the walls of the Mortimers' garden. Smythe had a map of Brightworthy and the land surrounding the village spread out on a picnic table. Grid-blocks on the map had been marked through, some crossed with two colors indicating the areas had been searched more than once.

Smythe handed Crowe a sheet of paper. "The volunteer's details, sir."

Crowe scanned the report, what little there was of it, and sighed.

"Absolutely squeaky," Burke said, reading over Crowe's shoulder.

"Indeed." Crowe handed the report to Burke. "And where is Mrs. Cicely Willington, age seventy-five?"

"This way, sir. The old dear's tucked up over here."

Crowe and Burke followed Smythe to a sunny patio where Mrs. Willington had been billeted in a lawn chair with a steaming cup of tea and the daily crossword.

"Nice work, Smythe," Crowe said.

Smythe's eyebrows did a little bounce. "Thank you, sir." He made introductions and left them to it.

"Mrs. Willington," Crowe said. "Thank you for your assistance."

"You're quite welcome, Chief Inspector. I'm glad to be of help. It's not often I get out in the field anymore."

Intrigued, Crowe asked, "Are you a retired police officer?"

Mrs. Willington, small-boned, her feathery gray hair swept back like wings on both sides of her head, reminded him of a mourning dove.

"Oh, goodness, no," she replied. "Nothing as official as that. I've been a civilian volunteer for years with the fire brigade and the neighborhood watch, but you know," she said, massaging her elbows, "time catches us up."

"Well, we're grateful you felt up to it today. Now, can you tell me exactly how you came to find the shoe?"

"Of course, I can, Chief Inspector—though it is a bit of a mystery. I've been over it in my mind and I cannot for the life of me figure it out."

"What can't you figure out?" Crowe knelt beside her.

"How I missed it the first time. Constable Smythe gave me that area because of my balance problem, you know. The ground isn't rough or bumpy back there."

"Yes," Crowe said, "Go on."

"It must be old age," she said, shaking her head. "I'm going gaga and not even aware of it. I passed that tree on the side closest to the garden wall. I looked closely, I know I did. There was nothing there. I made my way back and forth, back and forth, the way one's supposed to do, across the alley to the neighbor's garden wall. My attention didn't waver; I was most careful. I started back to report to

Constable Smythe that the area was clear and it was then I saw it, that little pink shoe shining like a beacon. It couldn't have been there before."

In some agitation, Mrs. Willington gripped the arms of the chair and pulled herself forward.

"It would have been impossible to miss it. Yet, clearly, Chief Inspector, I did miss it. And it is only because I went back that way that I saw it. I could have gone on down the alley. I almost did. But something made me go back to the Mortimers' garden wall. I've no idea why." She shook her head and eased herself back into the chair.

"Whatever the reason, it's our good fortune that you did. Now, can you tell me what time that was, Mrs. Willington?"

At Crowe's praise, she perked up immediately, eyes bright as a sparrow's. "Of course, Chief Inspector, I noted the time particularly. Because of the shoe, you know." She fiddled a small notebook from her pocket, followed by a pair of brightly colored reading glasses that she positioned and repositioned on her nose as she turned pages in her book. "Ah," she said at last. "I've got it. It was eight-thirty this morning, precisely."

"And when did you commence searching that area?"

"At eight o'clock on the dot."

Crowe thanked Mrs. Willington profusely. She was glowing like a peach as he and Burke walked back to the car.

"What do you make of that?" Burke asked. "The old girl's not gaga. Sharp as a tack, if you ask me. Two previous grid searches in an area that small, they wouldn't have missed a flea." Burke sipped from his carry-cup and made a face. "Nasty," he declared. He cracked open the door and dumped the cold coffee into the gutter.

"The same thing you're thinking, I expect," Crowe replied. "If Mrs. Willington didn't put the shoe there—and I don't believe for a minute that she did—who did?"

"And why? If she didn't put it there and she didn't miss it on her first pass, then it had to have been put there *while* she was searching the area. And the place crawling with police."

"That's the million-dollar question, Rolly." Crowe flipped open his tablet and logged in to his e-mail. "Has Waverly sent the MAPPA search?"

Burke checked his mobile. "Yeah. And it's not good news. There's a Level Three sex offender recently moved into the area."

"Who?"

"Arthur Tuttle. Lives in Williston."

Arthur Tuttle's registered place of residence squatted atop a ramshackle automotive garage. An open stair attached to the L-shaped end of the building led to the flat-roofed, low-ceilinged, waste-board affair. The look of the place made Crowe's skin crawl.

"He ain't up there, mate."

The voice sounded close, but Crowe saw no one.

"Police. Show yourself."

A man wearing a mechanic's coverall, pushing a tire in front of him, emerged from a door beneath the stair. No wonder they hadn't seen him, Crowe thought. He'd probably stayed hidden until he was certain they were looking for Tuttle and not him.

"What's your name?" Burke asked. "Let's see your identification."

"Keep your hair on." The mechanic shot them an aggrieved look.

"Get on with it," Burke snapped. "We haven't time to mess about."

"Keith Rickey." He leaned the tire against the stair before extracting a greasy-looking wallet from oil-stained coveralls. He handed Burke his license.

Scrawny, with nicotine-stained fingers and teeth, Rickey stank of strong tobacco and petrol.

Burke smiled benevolently. "We're looking for Arthur Tuttle. He gave this location as his address."

"Gotten himself into it again, has he?"

"What do you mean by that?" Crowe asked.

Rickey made a show of lighting a hand-rolled, unfiltered cigarette and took a long drag. He exhaled tendrils of smoke through his nose, pausing for effect, then sucked them back in.

"I know what he done. They say that type don't quit, even if you cut off their goolies."

Crowe pulled up a picture of Evie on his mobile and held it up in front of Rickey. "Have you seen this child here?"

Rickey paled. "No!"

"Would you tell us if you had?" Burke asked.

"Sure, I would," Rickey said. A look of understanding that turned to outrage spread across his face. "What, you think I'm like him?"

"He lives with you, doesn't he?" Burke asked.

"I don't live here. What do you take me for? Tuttle lives up there. He's a lodger." Ricky jerked a thumb at the stairs. "Where you was going when I saw you."

"You know what he's done and you rent to him?" Crowe asked.

"Not a crime. Besides, there ain't no kids 'round here. Better he's here than in some neighborhood."

"Well, Mr. Rickey, we'll see for ourselves whether your friend is here or not." Crowe moved toward the stairs.

"Look it, he ain't here. He's got a job he goes to."

"Where?" Burke said.

Rickey muttered something unintelligible under his breath.

"Sergeant Burke," Crowe said, "ring DI Waverly. Have her bring a team to Mr. Tuttle's flat. Make sure you're here to let my officers in, Mr. Rickey. If you're not, they'll break down the door."

"Now that we understand each other," Burke said, pulling out his mobile. "Be a good chap and tell us where to find Tuttle."

"He works at Peterson's News & Tobacco. Down this alley, cross, and turn left. You can't miss it."

"For your sake, I hope you're telling the truth." Crowe paused. "And, Mr. Rickey, do not alert Mr. Tuttle that we're on our way."

Rickey glowered at them. "Don't you be threatening me. He'll be there all right. And he ain't my friend."

As they started down the alley, Crowe heard a gob of spit hit the ground behind them. "Against the law," he said over his shoulder.

"Isn't everything?" came Rickey's sour reply.

Peterson's News & Tobacco had a steady stream of foot traffic.

"Blimey," Burke said. "What're they selling to get business like that?"

Crowe laughed. "I'd wager Peterson, if there is a Peterson, has a betting shop or some such set up in the back."

"No doubt," Burke said. "Look at the windows. They've painted the glass."

They crossed the road and went into the shop. The front was a maze of off-kilter spinners stuffed with newspapers, sporting magazines, and racing forms. Beyond these, Crowe saw racks of fitness and men's magazines. Burke directed his attention to a portable partition at the back with a hand-lettered placard on the door stating: Adult Videos ~ Under 21 Not Allowed.

Tuttle stood at a counter to their left. Embroiled in a verbal altercation with a couple of customers, he had not yet noticed them. With a derisive wave of his hand, he dispatched the disgruntled pair. When he saw Crowe and Burke, his face twisted in disgust.

"Not my day today. No, it bloody isn't," he muttered.

At the counter, Crowe reached for his warrant card.

"Don't bother," Tuttle said. "You could hardly be more bloody obvious."

Crowe winked at Burke. "We've been made, Rolly."

"Nice place," Burke said. He nodded toward the back where a group of men clustered around a display of adult magazines. They glanced uneasily over their shoulders.

Tuttle needed a shave. His hair and his shirt both wanted washing. In vivid contrast to the rest of him, Tuttle's hands were like a woman's—small, soft, and finely manicured. His nails shone like little moons from a recent buffing.

"I've been expecting you lot. You've got that tot's face plastered all over the county and her mum weeping and begging on telly."

"Shut it, Tuttle," Burke said.

Tuttle snorted. "You can't solve your little problem with me. I've got an alibi." He thrust out his jaw. "I was right here at my job and my employer with me, not to mention any number of customers will recall I handled their transactions."

"Do your friends have alibis?" Crowe asked.

Tuttle laughed bitterly. "Friends? What friends? You lot have made my life a misery. Can't get what I need no more and that's a fact. My life's a ruin and no mistake."

"We've been to your flat," Burke said.

Was that a flash of panic Crowe saw in Tuttle's eyes?

"You've no right to toss my place."

An edge had crept into Tuttle's voice. They were getting to him.

"Unfortunately, for you," Burke said, "because of your previous convictions, we can search your place any time we feel there's a need."

"And arrest you," Crowe said. "If we think you're lying to us or holding back information that would lead to the recovery of Evie Mortimer."

Tuttle's face had gone gray.

"She's your type," Burke said. "Are you denying it?"

"Let's look at your history, Arthur," Crowe said. "Violent, predatory pedophile ..."

"Shut your mouth," Tuttle hissed. "You're putting a target on my back."

Crowe noticed the men in the back had moved closer as their exchange with Tuttle became more heated. Burke held out his phone, displaying Evie's picture. "Oy, you lot. Any of you seen this little girl? Around here? Anywhere?"

They shook their heads and mumbled "no," "never seen her" as they retreated through the partition door.

Burke turned back to Tuttle. "Should I have look?

Tuttle's mouth twisted in a mocking smile. He sniggered. "It's filthy, but it ain't illegal."

Crowe slammed his fist on the counter. "Released from prison three months past. Moved to the Williston area three weeks ago. Surprise, surprise, little Evie Mortimer goes missing. And here we are, Arthur. Here we are. Wanting answers, Arthur. Answers only you can give us."

Tuttle gripped the edge of the counter, his face so close to Crowe's that Crowe nearly gagged on the man's breath. Earlier, he'd wondered about the crusty white residue around Tuttle's lips. Now he could see it was dried froth from chewable antacids used to treat the sour stomach causing Tuttle's halitosis.

Crowe held out his phone so Tuttle could see Evie's picture. Tuttle stared, then seemingly without realizing what he was doing, reached for the phone.

Crowe pulled back. Startled, Tuttle jerked his hand away.

"I swear, I never seen her except on telly."

Burke's mobile rang. He answered, then turned to Crowe and shook his head.

Tuttle grinned broadly. "You got nothing on me!" he exclaimed.

"Where's your guv?" Burke asked. "Let's get your so-called alibi sorted."

"He's not here," Tuttle said. "He has business elsewhere."

"You let him know," Crowe said, "he's got business at Killingsworth Constabulary within the hour. If he doesn't show, we'll be back for you."

"Oh," Burke said. "Our lads send apologies for the mess."

Tuttle gritted his teeth.

"I do hope you're not thinking of doing a runner," Crowe said. "That turned out rather badly for you the last time."

Burke smiled pleasantly. "Do yourself a favor, Arthur. Take us to Evie and we'll put in a good word on your behalf."

"Haven't got her," Tuttle spit out the words. "And you claiming I do won't make it so."

"Your name hasn't been mentioned in connection with Evie Mortimer." Crowe flipped open his mobile. "Yet."

In the Incident Room at Killingsworth CID, DI Waverly removed a snapshot of Evie Mortimer from the evidence board and replaced it with a portrait taken recently by a professional photographer.

"Evie has heterochromia iridum," Waverly said pointing to the girl's eyes. "In other words, she has one blue eye and one brown eye. It's a significant distinguishing feature. You couldn't see it on the other photograph, but it's unmistakable in this one."

"Well done, Waverly," Crowe said. Evie Mortimer had wispy red-gold hair, shoulder length.

Slightly parted lips revealed baby teeth. In the picture, she was wide-eyed. Crowe thought she looked surprised. Her features were burned in his memory. He could see her with his eyes closed. Last night, he'd dreamed of her, but she'd had his sister's face.

He turned to Smythe. "Have you found anyone who saw Evie leave with her family or return with them?"

"A couple across the street saw them pull in Sunday night, but couldn't say for sure if Evie was with them."

Crowe wrote on the evidence board.

"How about the caravan park where they say they stayed?"

"The manager can only confirm that the Mortimers' caravan was there the entire time. We're running the license plates of vehicles that registered around the same time."

Burke leaned back in his chair. "You don't believe the parents' story, guv?"

"Not entirely, no."

"Sir," Waverly said. "A Mr. Peterson stopped in to alibi Arthur Tuttle. But, it's only a partial alibi."

Smythe snorted. "Did you hear him going on about that scum, Tuttle, like he was a Boy Scout?"

"The search of his place turned up nothing," Waverly said. "There's nothing to connect him to Evie Mortimer. He's under surveillance."

Smythe made a face. "Peterson's News & Tobacco is a front for porno. Ten to one, Peterson's one of them."

Waverly frowned. "It's no good moaning about it."

Smythe took a deep breath. "It's Tuttle. You mark my words."

"Waverly, what does the forensic lab say about the shoe?" Crowe asked.

"Nothing yet, sir."

"We can't discount Tuttle," Smythe said. "He was part of larger ring that supplied custom orders."

"We're not discounting him," Crowe said. "Waverly, coordinate with the Yard's Pedophile

Unit. If they pick up anything in their surveillance, I want to know about it immediately."

"Yes, sir." She looked down at her keyboard and grimaced. "Ugh," she said. "The thought of it turns your stomach."

Crowe tapped the evidence board. "Evie's been missing forty-eight hours. Her mother appears to be the last person to have seen her. We found no forced entry of the Mortimers' home. Nothing has turned up on CCTV security cameras. The dozen reported sightings have all been false."

Crowe secured a picture of the pink shoe to the timeline. "And, as you all know, we've had no viable leads until today."

Waverly flipped through the Mortimers' statement. "Here it is," she said. "Karen reported those shoes missing, along with a green tulle sparkle-skirt, a yellow flower petal top, and a lion-head hat on the day Evie went missing."

Crowe drummed his fingers on the desk. "The clothing that Karen reported missing, what do you make of that?"

"Doesn't make any sense," Waverly said. "If someone took her out of her bed, why stop and dress her in a get-up like that. And, if the kidnapper didn't dress her, why take it along?"

Burke whistled softly. "Play time."

"Spot on, Sergeant," Crowe said. "Other than the shoes, those clothes were for playing dress up. They were in her toy box."

Waverly closed her eyes and sighed. "Evie dressed herself."

"Yes," Crowe said. "I believe she did." He stood up. "Sergeant Burke and I need to have another talk with the Mortimers. And let's do another canvas of the village. Someone, somewhere, knows something, saw something, or heard something. We just haven't found them."

Karen Mortimer answered the door. When she saw them, her eyes narrowed and her mouth formed a hard, tight line. Crowe didn't flinch. He asked to come in and she grudgingly stepped aside.

The lounge was a shambles. Newspapers, cups, glasses, and take away cartons littered every surface. Karen wedged herself into a space between an arm of the couch and a jumble of boys' sport socks and Y-fronts.

"Sit, if you can find a spot."

Crowe and Burke moved stacks of posters from two chairs and sat facing her. Gaunt-faced and puffy-eyed, Karen looked as if she'd lost weight since Crowe had last seen her; she'd been skinny as a twig then. She wore dirty white shorts and a pink, sleeveless top. She hadn't bothered to put on a bra and when she turned to roll the loose socks into balls, he could see the slight swell of her breasts.

With an exaggerated sigh, Karen shoved the clothes aside and grabbed a packet of cigarettes from a side table. She shook one out and tapped it on the side of her hand before lighting it.

"What do you want, Inspector?" She took a quick, anxious drag.

What did he want? He'd expected her first question to be: Have you found her?

She held up her cigarette. "I've started smoking again."

"Karen," Burke said, "do you have any idea how Evie's shoe came to be under the tree outside your garden wall?"

Karen looked confused. "What? ... I don't ... It must have fallen off when she was taken."

"How can that be, Karen?" Burke asked. He smiled encouragingly. "That area was searched twice before and the shoe wasn't there."

"It's obvious, isn't it?" a man's voice interjected. Karen's husband, Malcolm, came into the lounge. "Someone put it there."

Unruffled, Burke said, "Spot on, Malcolm. Do you know who that someone might be?"

"How the devil would I know who put it there?"

"There aren't that many possibilities given the short window of time and the fact there were police all around your house when the shoe appeared."

Malcolm gaped at them. "Now, just a minute!" he exclaimed. He began to pace. He turned on Crowe. "You think we had something to do with Evie's disappearance? You think we put the shoe there to make it look like ... look like ..."

"Look like what, Malcolm?"

"I don't know," Malcolm stammered, "like someone carried her off."

"Your words, Malcolm, not ours. Now, tell us about the shoe."

Malcolm snorted. "This is outrageous!"

"Don't be an idiot, husband dearest. We're suspects. We've been suspects all along, isn't that right, Chief Inspector?" Karen stared at Crowe steadily, silently challenging him.

"Unfortunately, that is why we're here."

Malcolm glared at them. "Get out!"

"We'll speak with the two of you again soon, Mr. Mortimer," Crowe said.

As they stood to leave, the front door opened and Ian, Evie's older brother, dashed in and skidded to a stop. He looked at his parents, then from Crowe to Burke. He mumbled a hello and headed for the stairs.

"Ian," Crowe said.

The boy stopped midway up the stairs.

"We know someone put Evie's shoe under the tree, but it would have been impossible for that person to put the shoe there without being seen, unless that person was already here and was known to the police. Did you put Evie's shoe under the tree, Ian, or do you know who did?"

"No," Ian said firmly and ran up the stairs.

Outside, Crowe saw a dark-blue, unmarked police vehicle parked opposite the Mortimers' driveway. Smythe and Waverly had started re-interviewing the neighbors. He and Burke would revisit residences where no one had been home during the first door-to-door.

Burke tugged at his tie and loosened it, then shrugged out of his jacket. He regarded the sweat stains on his shirt and harrumphed.

"Well, so much for that," he said, and pulled the jacket back on. "I'll take this end of the village shall I, guv, and you the other?"

Two hours later, at the next-to-the-last house on his list, Crowe found an elderly Mr. Ashford and his dog, a sprightly Jack Russell terrier, pottering about in the garden. He'd had a bad reaction to some medicine, he said, and had stayed a few days with his daughter in Williston. Fingers crossed, Crowe showed him Evie's picture. The old man took the photograph and held it at arm's length, scrutinizing. When he nodded and said he'd seen the Mortimer children, Crowe wanted to kick up his heels.

"The brother was in a confab with two boys about his own age, I reckon. They were in the front garden, if you can call it a garden, of the old Rutherford place. When they see us out and about, they want to play with Fezziwig."

"But not on that day?"

"No. Didn't wave. Didn't even look. The brother followed the two boys inside and the little girl went with them."

"How long did they stay inside?"

"Dunno. I didn't stop. None of my business."

"Did you see them again after that at any time?"

"Wasn't home again until today, as I said. Saw the news about her on the telly. Poor little mite. Hope you find her."

"We're doing our best," Crowe said. "Can you show me where you saw them?"

"Of course, just there," Ashford said, directing Crowe's gaze up the street to the right. "Third from the corner. You can't miss it. Been lowering the property values on this street for years."

There was a sight line, but no direct access between the Mortimers' home and the Rutherford house. DC Smythe's contact card was still stuck in the door. The other houses in the street had tidy, attractive front gardens. Here, the grass, suffocated by weeds, struggled to grow. The paint peeled. The shades on every grime-covered window were drawn. Ramshackle, Crowe thought, that was the word for it. He went up the cracked walk to the front door and knocked. No answer. He knocked again loudly. Nothing.

He pulled out his mobile and rang Killingsworth CID. Waverly answered and he requested she check the name of the property owner. He waited while she looked it up. "Be certain he has the keys with him."

Crowe followed a foot path to the back of the house where he found a cramped yard littered with broken-down furniture, a cracked aquarium, and a heap of broken boards, metal fittings, and broken glass. He picked his way through the refuse and peered into the aquarium. Open to the weather, rain had turned whatever was left inside to a foul-smelling sludge. Crowe wrinkled his nose. A couple of dilapidated lawn chairs sat on a concrete slab—a parody of a patio – at the bottom of the back steps. In a window well, Crowe noticed a broken window, large enough for a child to crawl through. He went up the steps and tried the door. Locked.

Thirty minutes or so later, a car horn tooted. Crowe rounded the side of the house and saw a middle-aged, unshaven, white man stepping out of DC Smythe's car. The man walked over to Crowe.

Crowe displayed his warrant card. "Detective Chief Inspector Crowe. And you are Mr. Rutherford, the owner?"

"Right. What's this about?"

"Do you live in this house, Mr. Rutherford?"

"Not no more. I let it out."

"To whom do you let it?"

Rutherford stared at Crowe as if he'd spoken an incomprehensible language.

"The name of your tenant, please, Mr. Rutherford."

Rutherford frowned, scratched the stubble on his chin and ran his fingers through his halo of uncombed gray hair. The question seemed to have flummoxed him.

"You collect the rent do you not?"

"You needn't take that tone. Give me a moment."

"While you're thinking, could you tell me the last time you had contact with your tenant."

This question seemed to further confuse Rutherford. Crowe suspected the man hadn't been to the property in a donkey's age.

"Barrett, maybe," Rutherford offered. "Might be Barstow."

"You'll have it written down somewhere, I'm sure," Crowe said.

Rutherford was having a good look round.

"The back is worse," Crowe said. "I'll be amazed if the neighbors haven't complained."

A vein pulsed in Rutherford's neck. He cleared his throat and spat. "How much is the fine?"

"I'm not here in that capacity," Crowe said tersely. "A three-year-old girl's gone missing. Evie Mortimer's her name. She lives at number 10 Birdbrook Lane. She was seen outside this house two days ago, right before she went missing."

"Why didn't you say so? No need to be so hush-hush about it. You want a look around, help yourself. You'll get no argument from me."

"Evie and her brother were seen going into this house with two other children." Crowe showed Rutherford Evie's picture.

"I don't know nothing about that. There ain't no children here. Whoever told you that has got it wrong."

"Unlock the door, please."

Rutherford trudged up the steps. The lock turned, but the door stuck and he had to force it back, dislodging a pile of uncollected post.

"Perhaps, we can discover the name of your tenant," Crowe said. He picked up a handful from the pile, sifted through it, tossed it aside, and picked up another handful.

"There's nothing but advertisements here. All of it addressed to Occupant. Did this person receive no post at this address?"

"How would I know?"

"Who did you rent to? A family? A single person?"

"A bloke."

"This bloke, any luck in recalling his name?"

"Blackwood, maybe."

"He signed a lease, didn't he?"

"We had a verbal agreement."

Rutherford stepped back through the open door. Crowe followed him and saw the Ford Mondeo coming up the street. Earlier, while waiting for Rutherford, he'd called his Sergeant for assistance. Burke parked and joined Crowe and Rutherford on the porch.

"Sergeant Burke, this is Mr. Rutherford, the owner."

Crowe turned to Rutherford. "Please wait in the Sergeant's car until we're finished."

Burke settled Rutherford in the backseat of the Mondeo.

Back on the porch, he watched Rutherford talking animatedly on his mobile. "Looks a bit dodgy to me."

"He's hiding something."

Half a dozen steps into the hall on the threadbare runner, they stopped abruptly. Crowe wrinkled his nose at the musky, armpit-like odor. "What is that smell?"

Burke shook his head. "No idea. Strong, though. Whew!"

They peered into rooms on either side of the hall. Brittle paper shades kept the rooms in shadow. Crowe felt along a doorframe for a light switch. He found one and flipped it on. The bulb was low wattage and provided only a dim light. It was enough for them to see the cracking plaster walls, the narrow floorboards, a couple of tatty throw rugs, a sagging couch, and a pair of rickety chairs. The lot of it looked like it had been picked off the street. Empty soda cans, crumpled cigarette packets, and other trash were scattered about. They found a similar scene in the room across the hall.

They moved on to the back of the house. In the kitchen, an Indian take-away meal had been set out on the table and abandoned untouched. Crowe saw the end of a receipt sticking out from beneath a flattened paper bag. He pulled it free and read the date. The food had been purchased the day before Evie Mortimer disappeared.

Burke raised an eyebrow.

"Take Mr. Rutherford to CID. Maybe that will improve his memory."

Crowe looked around the kitchen. No dishes. No pots and pans. In the pantry, he found a door with the knob missing, the hole plugged with a wad of newspaper. An open padlock hung from a hasp. Crowe tugged at the paper plug. The door opened easily onto steps going down into the darkness of a cellar. He felt inside the door for a light switch—found it and turned it on. Crowe descended cautiously. The hair on the back of his neck prickled; he felt a tremor in his bowels, a chill up his spine.

The basement was empty. Not so much as a shelf or a workbench. A thick coating of dust on the floor showed scuff marks and footprints going every which way. Crowe saw a narrow path in the dust. It appeared something had been dragged from one side of the cellar to the other. He followed the drag path to another set of steps that led up to the hatchway doors he'd seen earlier at the back of the house. He swiped at the cobwebs in the doorway, ducked his head, and went half way up the steps. He pushed on the doors and lifted them easily.

A short while later, Burke returned.

"Something happened here, Rolly." Crowe pointed to the hodgepodge of footprints. "Something was dragged out through those doors."

As they returned to the stairs, Crowe noticed something under the bottom tread. He used his pen to nudge it into the light. Burke pulled a latex glove from his pocket and picked up the chalky, white lump.

He made a face. "Oy, what a stink."

"Bag it," Crowe said. "And get a Scenes of Crime team out here."

Late that afternoon, when they returned to Killingsworth CID, Crowe was surprised to find Karen and Ian Mortimer waiting for him. Ian insisted on speaking with Crowe alone. Karen reluctantly agreed.

"I'll be right out there." She pointed at the visitors' area where they'd been sitting.

In the Interview Room, Crowe smiled in what he hoped was a warm, encouraging way.

"What is it you wanted to see me about?"

Ian sighed. "I've done something stupid." He paused. "I didn't mean for it to happen. It's just that sometimes I want to do stuff and not have to watch her, but mum always has a headache. She has to lie down a lot."

"Go on."

"I got up early. I wanted to watch telly. But Evie woke up, too. She wanted breakfast and she needed to be changed. Mum wouldn't get up. I think she took one of her pills."

Crowe's heart beat faster. "What happened?"

"I took her diaper off her and dressed her."

"Did you dress her in the sparkle-skirt?"

"Yeah. She's loves that stuff. And that goofy lion hat mum-mum bought her. Then I toasted a jam thingie for her. But she kept pestering me to take her outside to play. I didn't want to, so I got the baby alarm and put it on her so I could tell where she was." He reached in his pocket, pulled out a plastic receiver with an antenna and laid it on the table. "The other part's a pink teddy bear."

Crowe picked up the receiver and examined it.

Ian looked the picture of misery. "Someone forgot to latch the gate. That's how she got out. I tried the alarm over and over. It didn't work. All I found was her shoe." He pushed his chair back and stood up. "That's all I know."

"Sit down," Crowe said. "Did you throw Evie's shoe over the garden wall?"

Ian hesitated. "Yeah."

"Why didn't you tell your parents?"

Ian looked away and began scraping at his thumbnail.

"Well?"

Crowe let the silence stretch.

"Your mother has to be told."

Ian's head snapped up. "You can't tell her!"

Crowe brought Karen Mortimer to the Interview Room. She looked as if she hadn't showered or changed her clothes in days.

"Is something wrong?"

Crowe heard the apprehension in her voice. He took his pen from his pocket and fiddled it between his fingers.

"We now know how Evie's shoe came to be outside your garden wall and who saw your daughter last." He let that sink in. "It was Ian who threw Evie's shoe over the wall the morning it was found."

Karen stared at Crowe. "What?"

"The morning Evie went missing, Ian said he tried several times to wake you, but couldn't. He thought you might have taken a sleeping pill."

Karen's face flamed scarlet.

"He'd gotten up early to watch telly by himself. But Evie got up too and wanted him to play with her outside. He dressed her, fixed her something to eat, put a child locator alarm on her, and let her play in the garden by herself. Sometime later, he went looking for her and she was gone, except for the shoe. He tried to find her with the locator device. When he couldn't, he panicked and hid the shoe. When the searches began, he waited for an opportunity, then threw it over the wall."

It took Karen a moment to fully grasp what Crowe had told her.

"The child locator alarm?" She shook her head briskly. "It isn't Evie's. It was Ian's. He walked in his sleep when he was little. If he moved thirty feet from the receiver, it started beeping. We haven't used it in years."

"He couldn't get a signal and thought it was broken."

Karen put her face in her hands.

"I have more questions I need to ask Ian," Crowe said. "And I'd prefer if you were present this time, Mrs. Mortimer."

Karen stared at her son. "Well?"

Ian looked away and began scraping at his thumbnail again. "I'm sorry, mum."

"Sorry won't half do, now will it?"

He didn't answer.

"Ian," Crowe said, "can you tell me what you and your sister were doing at Mr. Rutherford's house the day before she disappeared?

The boy stared at the table; Crowe couldn't see his reaction.

"Where's that?" Ian asked.

Crowe described the location.

"Oh," Ian said. "We walked past it plenty times. But we never stopped."

"You never went there? Never talked to anyone?"

Ian shook his head. "No one lives there."

"What's this got to do with Evie?" Karen asked.

"Ian's not telling the truth. He and Evie were seen going inside." Crowe had the boy's attention now.

As Karen took in her son's reaction to Crowe's accusation, her demeanor changed. "Ian! What have you done?"

The boy looked as if she had struck him.

"Who were the two boys and why did you follow them into that house?" Crowe asked.

Ian said nothing.

"Answer!" his mother shouted.

Ian winced. "Just some kids. They were with their mum."

Crowe asked again, "Why did you follow them in?"

When Ian shrugged, his mother twisted his arm. The boy cried out. Karen glared at him. "Tell it," she said. "Right now!"

"Stop it, mum! I didn't mean for it to happen. It wasn't my fault!"

"What happened?" Crowe asked.

Ian hung his head. "They said the guy their dad worked for had snakes and lizards and stuff in there. I said I didn't believe it. And they said they'd prove it."

"And were there snakes and lizards?"

"Yeah."

"What happened when you went inside?"

"We were looking at the cobra. One of the kids was tapping on the glass. The cobra stood up and started striking at him. That's when the guy ran down from upstairs."

"What did he do?"

"He was yelling and swearing. I grabbed Evie and we ran. I don't know what happened to the other kids. I guess they got in trouble."

During Ian's revelation, Karen sat open-mouthed, stunned.

"What were you thinking, Ian?" She turned to Crowe. "Do you think these people took Evie?"

"I don't know," Crowe said. "We're looking for them. Ian and Evie may have seen something they shouldn't have."

"Oh, dear Lord, do you think Ian's in danger, too?"

Ian started to cry. Crowe felt for the boy. He'd been in a similar situation himself years ago. He put a hand on Ian's shoulder. He wished he could tell him it would be all right.

Crowe sat in his office at Killingsworth CID reviewing reports. He'd had another short, terse call that morning from Detective Chief Superintendent Parker-Bowles wanting to know why after ninety-six hours Crowe and his team had failed to find Evie Mortimer or recover her body. The public and the media, Parker-Bowles informed him, were snapping at their heels wanting information, answers, and he had nothing to give them.

Two days after Rutherford had identified his tenant as Terence Banks, Banks and a man named Dawson had been taken into custody. Rutherford, as Crowe suspected, knew more about the goings-on at his property than he wanted to tell. Banks had refused to speak without a solicitor. Smart fellow. But Rutherford, facing a charge of obstructing a police investigation, had revealed that Banks was a reptile smuggler. Rutherford, for supplying the "safe house," got a cut of Banks' profits on the illegal sale of the animals. Both vehemently denied any knowledge of Evie Mortimer. Crowe shut down his tablet and turned to his Sergeant.

"Banks isn't your run-of-the-mill reptile smuggler. His clientele are connoisseurs. Not satisfied with your average deadly viper. Generally speaking, he's a loner. But, based on what Rutherford let slip, I suspect he had a special order that required more than one man, hence, Dawson."

Burke leaned back in his chair. "You think they're lying?"

Crowe shook his head. "No. I believe they're telling the truth or as much of the truth as you can ever expect to get from that sort. When you think about it, Rolly, it doesn't matter what the Mortimer children saw, because Banks and Dawson vacated the property immediately with no intention of ever returning. They guessed, and rightly so, that Ian and Evie would keep quiet because they knew they'd get into trouble."

"We're back to nothing, then," Burke said.

Crowe heard the disappointment in his Sergeant's voice. The whole department had been working round the clock to find Evie. Now it seemed their only real lead had dried up. They had failed to find her. Failed to turn up one clue to her whereabouts. Crowe steepled his fingers and gazed at the ceiling fan that turned lazily overhead. "Unless something else happened."

"What are you thinking, guv?"

"It's unlikely we'll get much more from Banks or Dawson at this point. We need a different approach. Locate Dawson's wife and bring her in for questioning."

A few hours later, Tina Dawson sat in Crowe's Interview Room.

"After Banks chased the children away, what happened?"

"The bastard gave my boys a good shellacking. Not that they didn't deserve it. But that's my job, not his. He had no right."

"And then all of you left the house, is that correct?"

"No. I took the boys home. Dawson was to come home after he helped Banks with a delivery."

"What time was that?"

"I don't know. Some time that night."

"But Dawson didn't come home. Why was that?"

Tina looked past Crowe at the door. "I want to go. I've done nothing. You can't hold me."

"If we find out that this business has anything to do with the disappearance of Evie Mortimer and that you could have given us information that would lead to locating her and refused to do so, you'll be spending your time in the same place they're going."

Tina tried to give him a tough stare. She wasn't good at it. Crowe thought she didn't really have it in her.

"If it was one of your kids missing four days and you had no idea where he was, don't you think you'd want someone who might offer a lead to come forward?"

Tina's eyes misted over and she sniffed a bit. That put her right where Crowe wanted her. Whatever else she might be, she wasn't a neglectful or uncaring mother. Crowe handed her a tissue packet.

"Thanks," she said and blew her nose. "You know right where to twist the knife, don't you? Your job, right? I'll tell you then, but I don't know how it could possibly help you."

"Just tell me," Crowe said. "Let me decide."

Tina took a deep breath. "When Dawson called later that evening, he said they had a problem. A serious problem. I left my boys with my mum and went over there. When I got there, they were packing to leave—lock, stock, and barrel. When Banks found out that Dawson called me, he lost his mind. I thought he was going to murder us."

"What did Dawson tell you, Tina?"

"I've said too much all ready. Banks will kill me if he finds out."

"Banks is in prison. He can't hurt you."

Tina looked hard at Crowe. "One of those things got away. And before you ask, I don't know what it was. Dawson didn't tell me. He wasn't half making sense anyway. Banks was having fits. They were running about outside trying to find it, but they were afraid to draw attention."

"And they didn't alert the police because it was illegal. They might have done so anonymously."

"Dawson might have done that, Chief Inspector, but Banks isn't that kind. He'd cut and run, and the less said the better. As much as I hate to say it, Dawson is weak. He needs someone to follow and he never picks the right one." She shook her head sadly.

"Do you know what Banks was keeping locked up in the cellar?"

"What? No. I didn't know there was a cellar."

Crowe believed her. He told her to go. Her kids were raising hell outside in the hall, but as soon as they saw her they settled down and fell into line behind her. He watched as they disappeared into the stream of people coming and going from Killingsworth Constabulary.

That night, alone in his office, Crowe massaged his temples and forehead, attempting to ward off a headache. On top of everything else, he now had a second crime on his hands: an escaped reptile, species unknown. Probably poisonous. Loose in a village. The local Constable, Priddy, had been alerted. Crowe had contacted a herpetologist at a nearby college, who had agreed to help them locate the thing, if it could be located. Needle in a haystack, Dr. Wakefield had said. But he was game. He realized the danger. On a hunch, Crowe described the white, chalky stuff he and Burke had found in Rutherford's cellar. Wakefield said it sounded like it could be a urate—reptiles excreted nitrogen in the form of uric acid, which could be excreted dry—but he'd have to see it to be sure. Crowe drummed his fingers on the desk, damning the slowness of the forensics lab.

He could not shake the feeling that the Mortimer children's visit to the Rutherford house and Evie's disappearance the very next day were related. It was the strongest lead they had. He had shared his theory—what little of it there was—with his team. On the surface, the connection between the two events appeared tenuous, but it was the only thing that made any sense.

A few days later, at seven o'clock in the morning, Crowe was surprised and fearful when the police dispatch alerted him to an emergency call reporting a snake in a swimming pool at a private residence in Brightworthy. When he arrived at the house, a glaringly modern glass and metal monstrosity, there was no answer at the front door. After a quick look around, he found a path and followed it to the rear of the house. On the way, Crowe rang his Sergeant and then Wakefield.

At the back, he found a distraught woman and Constable Priddy standing near the terraced steps of a kidney-shaped swimming pool. Crowe identified himself and joined them, gazing into the sparkling water. What he saw there, lying at the bottom of the pool, deeply shocked him. He reckoned the pool to be at least fifty feet long. The snake, an albino Burmese python, stretched nearly half its length.

The middle-aged woman, wearing a white bikini, was soaking wet and shaking uncontrollably. Crowe looked from the woman to the Constable. Both she and the Constable appeared mesmerized.

"Constable Priddy," Crowe snapped.

The young officer jerked to attention. "Sir."

"Have you called Animal Control?"

"Yes, sir, they'll be here directly." He swallowed. "I'm to keep the snake from leaving the pool until they arrive."

Crowe eyed the creature. It hadn't moved. He knew a bit about pythons. They were crack swimmers and could stay submerged for as long as thirty minutes.

"I'll assist you," Crowe said.

The young officer looked much relieved.

Crowe nodded toward the woman. "Report, Constable."

Priddy flushed. "Sorry, sir. It's just that ... well ... as best as I can make out, Mrs. Trevanian came out at approximately six-thirty for her morning swim. She dove into the water at the other end of the pool and swam a couple laps before she noticed something on the terraced steps at this end. She had her glasses off and couldn't see clearly what it was from that distance. She moved closer and at that point the snake raised its head and she realized what it was."

Mrs. Trevanian groaned. She stared at Crowe, her eyes glassy bright. "It raised its head and looked right at me." She hugged herself tightly, but her body still shook. "I couldn't believe my eyes." She squeezed her eyes shut, as if trying to rid herself of the memory.

"It started to move, to uncoil." She made a strangled cry. "My god, there was no end to it. I couldn't scream. I couldn't move." She clapped a hand over her mouth. "And then I did scream. I know I did. And then ... I don't remember. Everything's a blur. But somehow, I got out."

Crowe saw her scraped knees, the abrasions on her thighs. She'd made it to the side and hauled herself out.

"And the snake?" he asked.

She pointed. "Down there, where it is now. Where I was." She began to cry.

Crowe slipped off his jacket and draped it around her shoulders. He led her away from the pool and settled her on a lounge chair while Constable Priddy kept an eye on the snake. If the python tried to leave the pool, Crowe had no idea how they would stop it. The only things at hand were two long-handled skims used for removing leaves and debris from the surface of the water. They would hardly do, except perhaps as a way to herd the snake back into the pool. Crowe was doubtful even of that. One only had to look at the thing to know it wouldn't work. The python at the bottom of Elspeth Trevanian's pool was at least twenty feet long and, even though the water magnified its size somewhat, Crowe had no doubt the creature had to weigh upward of two hundred pounds.

"Sir," Priddy called, his voice shrill. "It's moving!"

Crowe urged Mrs. Trevanian to go inside. Then he grabbed the skims and hurried to where Constable Priddy stood at the edge of the terraced steps.

Crowe handed Priddy a skim. "Stand well back. Pythons are fast and dangerous if threatened."

The snake's head broke the surface of the water. They retreated to what Crowe hoped was a safe distance. The python stared at them a moment, eyes cold and expressionless. Then it swam toward the steps.

The snake's body undulated as it sailed through the water and Crowe could not help but admire the grace with which the creature swam. Its massive size made its agility even more amazing. Confronted by Crowe and Priddy, the snake halted, raised its upper body, and extended its flat, blunt-nosed head. Its forked tongue flicked out, tasting the air between them. Crowe stepped forward and pressed the skim against the creature's neck. Its head whipped around and, in an instant, it lunged at Crowe. He scrambled back. The snake hissed, its mouth wide open. Crowe hit it with the skim pole.

"Priddy," he shouted. "I'll take this side, you take the other."

Hesitant at first, Priddy found his courage and came forward, his skim at the ready. Crowe felt for him. Police school couldn't prepare you for something like this.

"Together now," Crowe said.

They advanced on the giant serpent, shouting and beating at the ground. For an instant, Crowe feared it wouldn't yield. Then, with another fearsome, open-mouth hiss, it whipped its massive body backward into the water and dove to the bottom of the pool. As Crowe and Priddy leaned on their skims breathing hard, adrenaline pumping, a man lugging a large plastic crate and a snake hook came onto the patio.

"Brian Steele, Animal Control."

Crowe identified himself and Priddy.

"Where's the snake?"

Priddy pointed to the pool. Steele walked to the edge. "Jesus God!" He looked from Crowe to Priddy. "Bloody hell. You might have warned me."

Priddy colored. "Sorry."

Steele hitched up his trousers. Squinting at Crowe, he scratched the back of his sun-browned neck. "I'll call for a stun gun."

"Look out!" Priddy shouted.

The snake surged out of the water and over the shallow steps, forcing them to leap aside. In seconds, a third of its body had already reached the terrazzo tiles on the patio, while the bulk of it still slithered past them.

Steele signaled Crowe and Priddy. "When the tail comes by, grab it and hold on."

Priddy looked at Steele as if the man had lost his mind.

"I know what I'm doing," Steele said. He held up the snake loop. "I'll get this around her head."

Crowe watched as the python continued to move toward the patio. With a shock, he realized that Mrs. Trevanian had not gone inside. He shouted and waved his hands. She saw the snake moving toward her and began to scream.

Steele, who apparently had not seen the woman when he arrived, looked up, startled.

Mrs. Trevanian still screaming, jerked open the door to the glass-walled sunroom that let onto the patio and fled inside. Crowe heard the door slam and the lock click.

"Now!" Steele shouted. They grabbed the snake's tail and hung on while its massive body whipped back and forth as it tried to shake them off. A second later, it lunged at them.

Crowe felt the snake's power as its muscles rippled and bunched and knew they were in trouble. As Steele advanced on its head with his noose, the snake rolled away. The heaviest part of its body, nearly a foot in diameter, struck Crowe and sent him sprawling. Priddy, knocked off balance, threw out an arm to steady himself. But, with nothing but air to hold on to, he lost his footing on the wet tiles and slid under the snake's head.

"Priddy!" Crowe shouted as he leaped to his feet. Lunging with unbelievable speed, the snake struck, sinking its teeth into Priddy's face. Priddy screamed, eyes bulging in panic. A heartbeat later, the snake heaved its body onto his shoulders.

Crowe heard a shout. Wakefield had arrived and was running to assist Steele. As they strained against the python's weight, the herpetologist took hold of the snake's head, while Steele tried to prevent it from coiling around Priddy. A minute later, Crowe saw his Sergeant come through the gate.

The snake was still gaining ground. Crowe grabbed at the torch in Priddy's utility belt. As if reading Crowe's mind, Wakefield said, "It's no good trying to beat it loose. See if these people have any whiskey."

They were all grunting with the effort of holding off the python and Crowe feared if he let go, the tide of the battle would turn against them.

"Damn it, man." Wakefield shouted. "Get moving! Get as much of the stuff as you can! Hurry!

"Rolly!" Crowe shouted, breaking the spell riveting Burke's attention on the grotesque scene. "Find some whiskey!"

"Call for an ambulance," Steele shouted after him. "This man needs care!"

Crowe heard pounding. Burke shouting. More pounding. Then a crash and glass breaking. At every opportunity, the snake pulled its body closer, attempting to wrap itself around Priddy's chest.

"Hold her back," Steele said through clenched teeth. "She'll suffocate him."

The snake bunched its muscles and squeezed. Priddy squealed, followed by an awful strangling sound as he clawed helplessly at the snake's head.

"Steady on!' Wakefield shouted.

Crowe heard desperation in Wakefield's cry, but he also heard Burke shout, "Got it!"

Wakefield loosed his hold on the snake and Burke took his place. Wakefield snapped a skim pole in half. He grasped the snake's head, prying at its mouth with his fingers. Seconds ticked by and Wakefield couldn't budge its grip on Priddy.

"Bloody hell," Wakefield muttered. His biceps bulged and the tendons in his forearms strained with the effort. Then, in an instant, the snake's jaws parted and Wakefield thrust the piece of skim pole in the gap.

"Here!" Wakefield shouted. "Hold this. And mind you don't let it slip."

Burke grabbed the rod. The power of the snake's jaws had already begun to crush the hollow metal tube. Wakefield opened a bottle and began pouring the whiskey in the snake's mouth.

Crowe looked at Steele. His face showed the strain of holding off the monster. Sweat trickled into Crowe's eyes. They were all exhausted.

"Hang on, guv," Burke said. Crowe nodded.

Priddy was ashen, his body limp. "Priddy," Crowe said, "can you hear me?"

"Unconscious," Wakefield said. "Mercifully." He grabbed another bottle and poured. The snake's mouth opened. Its head reared backward.

"Now!" Wakefield shouted. "Drag it back!"

For a moment, Crowe thought the snake wouldn't budge, then it uncoiled, lashing from side to side. Finally, staggering under its powerful body, the four of them hauled the monster away from Priddy. With Wakefield controlling its head with a noose, Steele, Crowe, and Burke, positioned at intervals along the snake's body, managed to keep it prone. Crowe saw the bulge at the same time as the herpetologist.

"Ate recently," Wakefield said. "Something large by the look of it."

"Sergeant," Crowe said, holding out his hand.

Burke handed him the child locator device.

"Fresh batteries?"

Burke nodded and Crowe pushed the button that activated the transmitter.

They heard a muffled *Beep! Beep! Beep! Beep!*

Banks finally spilled on the python. He'd stolen it from a breeder in France. The job should have been a piece of cake. But it wasn't. From the start of it, nothing had gone right. His regular man had been bitten, nearly killed. He'd had to take on Dawson at the last minute. It was his bad luck the snake had started to shed while they were smuggling it into England. Painfully uncomfortable, the twenty-foot foot albino burm was aggressive and hungry. Banks had told Dawson how to contain it, how to take care of it, had given him precise instructions. But the lazy git hadn't done as he was told. And the snake, to no one's surprise except Dawson's, had escaped. Pushed through the unsecured cellar hatchway doors and disappeared into the night and the lush gardens of Brightworthy.

"And you didn't report it because it was stolen, is that right?" Crowe asked.

"That's right." Banks laughed without mirth. "I'm no fool."

"That monster killed a three-year-old child. Dawson, to his credit, is devastated. But you, you care nothing about that, do you?" Crowe did not try to hide his disgust.

Banks stared steadily at Crowe.

"That snake was worth £42,000. I had a buyer. And now, because of that toerag Dawson, I have no snake, no money, and you've clapped me in irons."

Crowe persisted. "You could have reported it anonymously. Why didn't you?"

Banks' eyes narrowed, a half smile tweaked his lips. "Now, where's the fun in that, mate?"

Excerpt from forthcoming novel,

Rag and Bone
A DCI Rylan Crowe Mystery

Chapter One

Pinkwater's Yard

Up by the road where Reg Pinkwater parked the Bradley, the slanting rays of the sun still blazed. He followed the path as it descended through the trees. Long shadows were already creeping towards day's end. The wood was still, almost silent, the only noise the occasional patter of a falling leaf or a green acorn thudding to ground. A light breeze from the river carried the trill of a nightingale. The scuffing of his feet along the path sounded rude by comparison.

He stopped at the gate of his father's old scrap yard. The property had been in Pinkwater's family long before his father began using it to shift salvage.

There were five acres of wood with a little under an acre cleared and fenced, as well as the two sheds and a makeshift hut. One shed housed his father's tools and the Bradley, which Pinkwater now drove. The other sheltered wood and iron work from the weather. In his father's day, the land had been part and parcel of a larger wood. Now, "Pinkwater's Yard" was surrounded by sport parks, self-catering tourist cottages, and a private fishing lodge. A prime piece of real estate, the land would be snapped up the moment it was offered for sale. When he'd hit upon the scheme to lure Swit to the property by offering him the opportunity to agent the sale, he'd had the yard cleared of the trees and underbrush that had overrun it.

Pinkwater wrenched the key in the weather-stiffened padlock, then put his shoulder against the frame and shoved the gate open. He rarely came here and never alone. Today there would be a reckoning. He and Swit, face to face, for the first time since ... since ... that day. And, he held in his hand the thing that would give him power over the man. The envelope contained one still shot from the video Buttergut had given him. It didn't appear to be much of anything, just a picture of Swit and a boy. But,

Swit would recognize it for what it was, where it came from, what it meant.

Pinkwater looked up into the canopy at the sunlight glinting among the swaying branches. He checked the time on his mobile. Swit would be arriving soon.

He gritted his teeth and crossed the yard to the makeshift hut like a horse in blinkers. The hut was built from odds and ends of lumber, the doorway covered with a drape of ragged leather. He shoved the skin aside. In the dim light that filtered through the plastic sheeting that covered the windows, Pinkwater recognized the rickety table covered in sticky lino, the old wood burner, and the ugly, crudely carved antique chair that the elder Pinkwater had straddled like a grotesque throne. Here he'd sat through the nights by the light of a single candle swilling homemade gin from a stained railway cup, while his family prayed he'd drink himself senseless. There, too, was the perilous camp stove, glass jars once filled with kerosene suspended beneath a flimsy metal frame cobbled together with wire, where his father cooked and ate his potted meats. The old man must have had the devil's own luck,

Pinkwater thought, not to have set himself ablaze with that monstrosity and the whole yard with him.

He ducked his head and stepped through the doorway. Inside, the heat and humidity settled over him like a shroud. The stinking air lay heavy on his chest, smothering his breath. Pinkwater turned on his heels and flung himself outside. He stood, breathing deeply, until he'd cleared the reek from his nostrils.

When it came time to hand Swit the agreement of intent, Pinkwater would hand him the envelope instead. How would Swit react when he realized he'd been caught out? It was never the same. Some ran, some cried, some begged, some fought. Pinkwater patted the pistol beneath his shirt. Whatever happened he was ready.

He turned away from the hut, didn't avert his eyes quickly enough and saw it, the hump of earth that marked his father's old refuse pit. Rubbish that defied even his father's cunning was dumped there. Every nerve protesting, Pinkwater forced himself to walk around it.

He could hear their voices still, taunting him. Stinkwater they called him and worse. Kids from his school, led by Swit, stalking him, following him to his father's yard, trapping him in a circle, firing acorns at him until his bloodied face stung like he'd been set upon by a swarm of bees. When he'd tried to break through their gauntlet, they knocked him down, kicked him, spit on him. Then they ran about whooping and shouting. He thought they'd finished with him, until Swit's triumphant cry echoed through the oaks. He had discovered the pit.

They dragged him to the hole and dumped him in. Their jeering and cursing drowned out his cries. They kicked viciously at the edges of the pit; dirt and stones rained down on him. Then, while he choked on dirt and wiped the grit from his eyes, the bastards unbuttoned their trousers and pissed on him. "Stinkwater," they shouted, "Stinkwater." He would never forget Swit's face, convulsed, lips twisted in a demonic grin, eyes blazing.

He cowered, terrified, listening to the frenzy of shouting and laughter above him. A stone struck his stomach. A board crashed down next to his head. A piece of rusted iron struck his leg. The maelstrom of debris they hurled down seemed endless until something sharp struck his temple. Lights like fireworks exploded in his eyes, then darkness.

When he came to, nauseous and addled, the silence was more terrifying than their blood-hungry shrieks or the awful knowledge they'd gone away and left him.

The sound of a horn hooting released him from the sickening reverie. The past, his past, had gripped him with terrifying power. He had sweated through his clothes. That a memory could incapacitate him was intolerable. His rage at Swit left him shaking. Nothing would do except Swit's utter destruction. He would strip him of his life and assets. Bleed him until he had nothing and no one he could call his own. He would hang him out naked for all to see, every ugly blemish in full view.

He must get up to the road, but to do that he had to cross the yard. The old fear held him back. Anger swirled in his head like a red mist. He would not stand for it. Reginald Pinkwater feared no man. He was no longer that child, helpless at the hands of cruel and careless classmates. He cursed and pummeled the air as if he could drive the demons away with his fists. He kicked at a stone, and then headed back to the path.

A few yards from the gate, he heard a sound – not the wind, he thought, not an animal. Could it have been a car passing on the road? Wary now, Pinkwater paused and stood motionless scanning the area. No movement. No sound. The hair on his neck prickled. He was being watched. He could feel it. He hunched down and headed for the gate at a trot. Pinkwater cursed under his breath. Idiot that he was, he had allowed himself to be caught up in the past, obsessing about Swit.

He stopped. Of course, it must have been Swit he'd heard. Now he felt a fool. But if it was Swit, why hadn't the man appeared? The niggling feeling of doubt swelled to a hot rush of paranoia.

He heard a shuffling behind him. Something small and hard struck his shoulder.

He spun around.

There were four of them, tall, heavy, with sacks over their heads. They watched him through jagged holes ripped in the fabric.

One of them raised his arm and light blazed into Pinkwater's eyes. He turned and another torch was turned on him, then another, and another as powerful as the first. The wattage was brutal; it was like staring into the sun. He was surrounded; no matter which way he turned the lights were there, needle bright, stabbing into his eyes. He shut his eyes. Then they rushed him. He struck out blindly, swinging his powerful arms in arcs around his body. His fists sunk into one of them. He heard the air rush from the man's lungs and with another punch knocked him aside. Pinkwater opened his eyes, flung himself through the breach and rolled across the ground. He reached under his shirt for his pistol.

"Shit!" one of them yelled. "The bastard's got a gun."

Pinkwater's lips curled in a sneer. "Alright you bastards, let's go!" he roared. He began firing and charged headlong into the light.

There was a yelp of pain, then another. He saw them scatter. They were shouting, cursing. The beams of light swung wildly about. They were trying to get behind him again. He swung around firing, and then his foot caught on something and tripped him. He crashed to his knees and they were on him. The pistol was kicked from his hand. Something large and heavy smashed into the back of his head.

His glasses went flying. Sparkles of red light exploded in his eyes.

When next he opened his eyes, he found himself in complete darkness. He lay still. He heard nothing but his own ragged breathing. Had they left him? His head ached ferociously. Toes moved, fingers flexed, not without pain, but they worked. His ankles were bound, wrists the same. The liquid trickling through his hair was blood; he was sure of that. He could smell it.

Pinkwater knew he had a concussion. He was disoriented and having trouble thinking clearly. A burst of panic churned his stomach. Was he blind? He blinked to clear his eyes and triggered another burst of pain in his head. He could feel the panic rising. There was no room for panic. Panic got you killed. Panic and you died. He swallowed a groan. If his attackers were still around, he did not want to broadcast that he was conscious. He closed his eyes and tried to make sense of what had happened to him.

He came to with a jolt. He heard voices, footsteps approaching. He'd passed out again. They were beside him now. He heard a tearing sound and the lights were back searing into his eyes. Pain wracked his head. He realized the tearing sound was a zipper being pulled open. Adrenaline flooded his veins; his heart beat frantically. Had they put him a body bag?

Something heavy dropped on his chest and the zipper was hastily dragged shut. He heard a low, ominous growl. They'd chucked an animal in with him. The creature turned in a circle on his chest, then clambered across his nose and mouth, its claws tearing at the corner of his eye. He screamed. Sweat ran from every pore. As he tried clumsily with his bound hands to dislodge the creature from his face, his attackers began slapping at it from outside. The animal howled and dug its claws into his scalp. They beat harder and faster. The enraged animal loosed his scalp and rolled about kicking wildly, digging its claws into his side. Claws raked his hands shredding skin and flesh. He smelled urine and felt hot liquid gush down his chest, then another worse smell, shit. It scrambled over him, fangs biting through his nose, his ear. A claw cut a gash across his eyeball. Unable to stop himself, Pinkwater shrieked.

Then just as suddenly as it began the slapping stopped. The zipper was torn open again and Pinkwater felt the claws puncture his thigh as the animal pushed away from him and leapt from its prison.

He opened his mouth to speak, but the sounds dissolved into an anguished groan. As soon as the sound escaped him, the first blow slammed into his head; then another in his side, and another between his legs. A boot smashed down on his face crushing his nose. Pinkwater moaned. There was no part of him now that was not in pain. He heard a voice ... the sound of the voice ...

"Twist," he mumbled, lips torn, tongue swollen. "Twist ..."

©2017 JM Reinbold

Acknowledgements

My thanks and gratitude go to Ramona DeFelice Long for her sharp eye and insightful prepublication edits; Justynn Tyme for his eye-popping cover illustration and design; Weldon Burge and Smart Rhino Publications, my first publisher; my critique partners in the Written Remains Mixed Genre Critique Group who never miss a single thing; early readers Gail Husch and Maria Masington for their invaluable insights; and Lois Hoffman, all-knowing publishing consultant. This book would not have been possible without all of you.

About the Author

JM Reinbold is the author of the DCI Rylan Crowe Britcrime mystery series. She is also a poet, editor, and the Director of the Written Remains Writers Guild. She lives in Wilmington, Delaware. Her fiction, essays, articles, and poetry have appeared in numerous anthologies and magazines, and on blogs and websites, as well as being nominated and selected for awards, grants, and literary fellowships.

Keep in Touch

Website: www.jmreinbold.com

Facebook Page: JM Reinbold

Amazon Author Page: J. M. Reinbold

About the Cover Artist

The cover art, like the story, is not what it seems. This realistic scene of an ominous and foggy English village was not staged. It was created from thousands of unrelated pieces to create the mood to match the mystery.

Justynn Tyme is a Buddhist, Dadaist, and a multi-talented experimental artist. He is currently the Director of the *All-Out Monster Revolt* project, a member of the *Written Remains Writers Guild*, and steward of the *Dada Network*. His work has appeared in both national and international publications. Justynn lives in Dada, Delaware—where he believes himself to be a ten-foot tall eggplant from outer space—with eight cats and a liquor cabinet in a house born yesterday.

Anyone interested can discover more by visiting... Justynntyme.com